THE GHOST OF CAMP WHISPERING PINES
by Susan Korman

Illustrations by
Gabriel Picart

Spot Illustrations by
Rich Grote

MagicAttic Club

MAGIC ATTIC PRESS

J
Kor

Published by Magic Attic Press.

For more information contact:
Book Editor, Magic Attic Press, 866 Spring Street,
P.O. Box 9722, Portland, ME 04104-5022

First Edition
Printed in the United States of America
1 2 3 4 5 6 7 8 9 10

Betsy Gould, Publisher
Marva Martin, Art Director
Jay Brady, Managing Editor

Edited by Judit Bodnar
Designed by Cindy Vacek

Library of Congress Cataloging·in·Publication Data

Korman, Susan.
    The ghost of Camp Whispering Pines / by Susan Korman ;
illustrations by Gabriel Picart ; spot illustrations by Rich Grote.
        p.   cm. -- (Magic Attic Club)
    Summary: During another adventure with the magic mirror the
members of the Magic Attic Club find themselves at summer camp on a
scavenger hunt that may lead them to a ghost.
        ISBN 1-57513-120-X (hardcover). -- ISBN 1-57513-119-6 (paperbound)
    [1. Camps--Fiction. 2. Treasure hunts--Fiction. 3. Ghosts-
-Fiction.]   I. Picart, Gabriel, ill. II. Title. III. Series:
Magic Attic Club (Series)
PZ7.K83693Gh 1998
[Fic]--dc21   98-2602
                                                           CIP
                                                            AC

As members of the
MAGIC ATTIC CLUB,
we promise to
be best friends,
share all of our adventures in the attic,
use our imaginations,
have lots of fun together,
and remember—the real magic is in us.

Alison   *Keisha*

Heather   *Megan*

Rose

Table of Contents

Prologue

When Alison, Heather, Keisha, and Megan find a gold key buried in the snow, they have no idea that it will change their lives forever. They discover that it belongs to Ellie Goodwin, the owner of an old Victorian house across the street from Alison's. Ellie, grateful when they return the key to her, invites the girls to play in her attic. There they find a steamer trunk filled with wonderful outfits—party dresses, a princess gown, a ballet tutu, cowgirl clothes, and many, many, more. The girls try on some of the costumes and admire their reflections in a tall, gilded mirror nearby. Suddenly they are transported to a new time and place, embarking on the greatest adventure of their lives.

After they return to the present and Ellie's attic, they form the Magic Attic Club, promising to tell each other every exciting detail of their future adventures. Then they meet Rose Hopkins, a new girl at school, and invite her to join the club and share their amazing secret.

HOT, HOT, HOT!

I'm so hot!" Megan Ryder moaned to her four best friends. She stopped her bike for a second and reached for her water bottle. After she'd gulped down a drink, she took off her bike helmet and poured a little more over her head. The cool liquid felt wonderful as it trickled down her long, strawberry-blond hair and onto her flushed face.

Alison McCann braked next to Megan. "I think it's hotter today than it was yesterday," she said, shielding her blue eyes from the blazing afternoon sun. "As soon as we get to the pool, I'm diving right into the water."

"Me, too!" Keisha Vance chimed in, zipping past Megan and Alison on her blue ten-speed.

Megan laughed. "That's what you two have been saying practically every day this summer. You're always the first two in the water."

It was a little after two o'clock on an August afternoon. Megan, Alison, and Keisha—along with their friends Rose Hopkins and Heather Hardin—were riding their bikes to the community pool at Overbrook Park. It had been an especially hot summer, and it seemed to Megan as if she and her friends had spent almost all of it at the pool.

I love to swim, Megan thought, placing the bottle back in her bike rack. I just wish we had thought of something else to do today. This seemed to happen every summer. By the time August rolled around, Megan started to get a little bored with hanging around at home and at the pool.

The girls turned into Overbrook Park. Heather locked up her bike, then adjusted the pink baseball cap that covered her hair. Her brown eyes took in the rows of cars jammed into the lot. There were even dozens of cars parked on the grass."I guess we weren't the only ones who decided to go swimming," Heather said to her friends.

"I guess not," Alison agreed. She slung her backpack over one shoulder, then led the way to the deep end of the Olympic-size pool. As they drew closer to the diving board, Alison noticed a group of people standing along the sides, all cheering wildly.

"Okay, swimmers, on your mark!" a lifeguard shouted through a megaphone.

Rose pulled her long, shiny black hair away from her face and craned her neck to see what was going on. The pool had been roped off into lanes. As the lifeguard blew his whistle, four swimmers dove into the water and began stroking toward the other end.

Rose turned to face her friends. "No wonder it's so crowded! The swim team is having a meet."

"We're not going to be able to go in until later," Heather remarked.

"We could go to the kiddie pool," Megan suggested halfheartedly.

"No way." Keisha shook her head firmly. She was wearing a light T shirt that set off her dark skin and eyes. "I'm not swimming with a bunch of little kids," she informed her friends. "I spent all morning baby-sitting

Ronnie and Ashley."

"Oh, right," Rose said. She remembered that both of Keisha's parents had been very busy at their jobs lately, leaving Keisha to spend a lot of the summer taking care of her younger brother and sister.

"Does anyone have any other ideas about what we can do?" Megan asked.

"We could go to the movies," Rose said.

"Hey! That's a good idea," Heather replied. "The theater is air-conditioned."

"I'm kind of sick of the pool anyway," Alison said.

"Me, too," Megan agreed, relieved that she wasn't the only one. "It's so weird," she went on. "Two months ago I couldn't wait for summer vacation to start. But lately..."

"Now, now, Megan!" Alison said, teasing her. "Don't tell me that you're actually looking forward to going back to school!"

Megan just smiled and shrugged as she followed her friends back to the bike rack. She didn't want to admit it, but a part of her was eager for school to begin. At least then she wouldn't be hot and bored anymore.

"Really? It's sold out?" Keisha stared at the woman in the ticket booth in dismay. "Are you sure there aren't any seats left for the movie?"

The woman nodded. "I'm positive, honey. It's so hot

lately; everyone's been coming to
the movies."

"Is anything else playing?"
Megan asked politely.

"*Chimps in Action* starts in
five minutes. It's very funny,"
the woman replied.

Alison shook her head.
"Thanks, but we already saw that."

Megan looked up at the board
where the movie titles were posted. The only other
possibility was something called *Two on the Run*, which
had started thirty minutes earlier.

"I guess the movie isn't going to work out, either," she
said to her friends in a defeated tone.

As the girls trudged back to the rack where they'd
parked their bikes, Rose noticed a sign in front of
Harborview Bank flashing the temperature: ninety-eight
degrees.

Yikes, she thought, we'd better think of something to
do before we all melt!

Just then another sign caught Rose's eye: ICY DELIGHT.
"Anybody in the mood for ice cream?" she asked.

"I'm always in the mood for ice cream," Keisha declared.

The girls headed for the ice cream parlor down the street.

Licking their cones, the girls started walking back to

their bikes. Overhead, the sun burned brightly, making them squint. They sat down on a bench to try to figure out how to spend the rest of the afternoon.

"We could go rollerblading," Heather suggested.

"No, thanks. I'd melt faster than this ice cream," Keisha replied, wiping a large drip from her chin.

"I'd invite you over to my house," Alison said, "but my brother Mark is having a Ping-Pong tournament in the basement and I promised we'd stay away."

"We ought to be able to think of something to do," Rose murmured. "After all, we're the Magic Attic Club."

Alison smiled at that. The five girls were not only best friends; they called themselves the Magic Attic Club because they shared a wonderful secret. Whenever they visited the attic at their friend Ellie Goodwin's house, they were transported on an adventure into a new place and time.

Thinking about the Magic Attic Club suddenly gave Alison an idea.

"I know what we can do!" she cried. She shot up from the bench like a rocket ship blasting off from its launchpad. "We can visit Ellie's attic!"

Megan blinked at her. "That's a great idea, Alison," she

said. "We can go on an adventure together."

"It sounds perfect to me," Keisha chimed in. She shook her head and laughed. "Can you believe it took all day for one of us to think of visiting the attic?"

Rose laughed, too. "Let's go, guys," she said, getting on her bike.

Heather was the only one who hadn't said anything about Alison's idea.

"What's the matter, Heather?" Alison asked, concerned. "Don't you want to go to Ellie's?"

"I'd love to go," Heather replied enthusiastically. "It's just that…it'll probably be about a million degrees up there," she reminded her friends.

Rose shook her head. "Guess what?" she said. "My grandfather helped Ellie install a window fan up there last week."

"That's good," Heather replied with a sigh of relief.

"And don't forget, Heather," Keisha reminded her with a secretive smile, "we don't have to *stay* in the attic!"

Within minutes the girls were back on their bikes, pedaling toward Primrose Lane.

Chapter Two

UPSTAIRS IN THE ATTIC

Ellie?" Megan called out softly. The five members of the Magic Attic Club stood on the steps that led onto Ellie's porch. Their silver-haired friend lay on a white wicker lounge chair, her eyes riveted on the thick book in her lap.

"Ellie?" Rose called her again.

There was still no reaction.

Keisha giggled. "She doesn't even know we're here," she whispered. "She's too busy reading."

"I'll get her attention," Alison said. "With three brothers at home, I'm used to making a lot of noise."

Alison cleared her throat, then yelled, "Hi, Ellie!" in a loud voice.

"Oh!" This time Ellie jumped, sending the book on her lap sailing to the floor. "Oh my goodness," Ellie gasped, looking up. "You girls startled me!"

Alison instantly felt bad. "I'm sorry, Ellie," she said, stepping onto the porch. "I didn't mean to scare you."

"We were just trying to get your attention," Heather chimed in.

Ellie smiled and smoothed her French braid. "I was so wrapped up in my book, I was completely oblivious to the rest of the world."

"What are you reading, Ellie?" Megan asked.

Ellie bent down to pick up the book. "It's called *Midnight Secrets.*"

Megan instantly recognized the book's title. "My mom and Aunt Frances read that a few weeks ago. They liked it so much, they lent it to everyone—my grandparents, my dad, our mail carrier..."

"My parents were talking about that book, too," Keisha said. "They said it was great."

"It is," Ellie agreed. "It has wonderful characters, and a very suspenseful plot. It's about a female detective who inherits an old mansion near the sea. Shortly after she moves in, she discovers that it's haunted."

"Woooo." Alison made a ghostly sound.

"That sounds pretty creepy, Ellie," Heather said, intrigued.

"The story is certainly very gripping," Ellie replied, with a nod. "The librarian recommended it to me yesterday. I haven't been able to put it down since."

"I love books like that," Rose said.

"So do I," Megan said wistfully.

"I know exactly what you mean," Ellie agreed. "There's nothing as pleasurable as losing yourself in a good book." Then, fixing her bright blue eyes on the girls, she changed the subject. "What have you girls been up to?"

"Not much," Alison replied.

"We've been really bored today," Keisha explained.

Ellie looked surprised. She set down the book. "Aren't you enjoying your summer vacation?"

"It's been great, but…we're getting kind of sick of the pool," Megan explained. "And then we couldn't get into the movies—"

"Or think of anything else fun to do," Heather added.

Ellie nodded as if she understood, and her eyes lit up. "Why don't you girls pay a visit to the attic?" she suggested. "I'm certain that would cure your boredom."

The girls of the Magic Attic Club exchanged grins.

"That's exactly why we came over," Rose told Ellie. "We wanted to take another adventure together."

"Is it really okay, Ellie?" Megan asked.

"Of course it's okay," Ellie replied. She waved them inside the house while she settled comfortably against the wicker lounger with her book. "You know where to find the key," she said."I'll be right here reading when you return."

Keisha inserted the gold-scrolled key into the lock and pushed open the door to the attic. The upstairs room was warm and quiet. The only sound Keisha heard was the faint whir of the window fan as it stirred the hot summer air. She could smell the scent of cedar mixed with something sweet. Lavender, Keisha guessed.

Rose reached up and pulled the tasseled cord that hung from the ceiling lamp in the middle of the room. As the attic filled with light, the girls hurried over to the old steamer trunk. Together Heather and Megan lifted the heavy lid.

Immediately, a long, flowing robe spilled over the side of the trunk.

Alison noticed a magenta magician's tuxedo with sequined lapels. "Rose, is this what you wore in your magician's adventure?"

"Yes." Rose's eyes glowed as she remembered her adventure as a famous magician's assistant. "It was so much fun!"

The girls sifted through the clothing, pulling out dozens of outfits as they tried to decide what to wear. Just then Rose noticed a rolled-up red sleeping bag. As she lifted it out of the trunk, a navy blue dress with red-and-white stripes caught her eye. Underneath the dress was a pair of red shorts and high-top sneakers.

"This stuff looks sort of interesting," Rose said. But as soon as she said the words, she felt a little unsure of herself. Rose was the newest member of the Magic Attic Club, and she was still getting used to the way the attic worked.

"Where do you think we'd go with that sleeping bag?" Heather asked curiously.

"I don't know," Keisha replied, jumping to her feet. "But do you see this?" she went on, picking up a red-hooded sweatshirt that zipped in front. "I'm ready to go somewhere cool enough to wear it!"

"Me, too," Rose said, pleased that her friends were interested in the items she'd found. She quickly slipped on the dress while Heather put on a pair of cutoff jeans, a

sweater, and red-and-white sneakers.

"I want to wear that skirt!" Megan said, eyeing a white denim skirt and a striped collared shirt that went with it.

After Alison had chosen shorts, a T shirt, and a colorful vest, Keisha hoisted the sleeping bag onto her shoulder. "I think we're ready, " she called out. Then she and her friends hurried over to a tall mirror that stood in the room. As they stared at their reflections, the walls of Ellie's attic seemed to melt away.

Chapter

Three

THE CAMPFIRE

ow," Megan heard Alison whisper. "Look where we are!"

Megan looked around eagerly. She and her friends stood in a forest of towering trees. Above them the sky was bright blue, and the air smelled like pine.

"Where are we?" Rose murmured.

"I'm not sure," Alison replied. "But it's *so* beautiful here."

"And so shady!" Heather chimed in happily.

"I told you I was ready to wear this sweatshirt!"

Keisha exclaimed.

The others laughed. They were all glad to be away from the scorching heat of the last few weeks.

Curious, Megan looked around. In a clearing just beyond the pine trees, she saw a sparkling blue lake. Several canoes and large rubber tubes were tied to a wooden dock that jutted into the water. In the western sky, an orange sun was slowly sinking behind a small mountain peak.

Keisha wandered closer to the lake. "I think we're at a camp, you guys," she said. She pointed to a small sign posted near the lake. Printed at the top were the words: SWIMMING AND BOATING RULES FOR WHISPERING PINES CAMPERS.

"A camp!" Alison echoed, as the girls joined Keisha. "This is great! We can go boating, hiking, swimming..." She ticked off all the fun activities on her fingers.

"I think we should explore some more before we do anything," Rose said. She noticed a dirt path that wound around the lake, then turned off into another section of the forest. "Let's try walking that way."

With Rose in the lead, the girls followed the trail. As they headed deeper and deeper into the forest, the air grew cooler and the sky seemed darker. Megan couldn't help thinking about the fairy-tale characters Hansel and Gretel wandering through the dense forest, lost. It would be easy for us to get lost here, too, she thought.

The Campfire

Before long the trail ended at a clearing. Six cabins stood in a semicircle, the tall pines looming over them like guards. Beyond the cabins, Heather could see a low, rectangular building marked REC HALL, along with several tennis courts, an area for archery, and a volleyball court.

"There's so much to do here!" Keisha said, amazed.

"I know. But…" Alison suddenly felt disappointed. The sun was already setting, and soon it would be dusk. "I wish we'd gotten here a little earlier. Then we could do more—"

"Alison! Keisha! Rose!" An unfamiliar voice cut her off.

Alison looked up. Two girls dressed in shorts and T shirts were coming out of one of the cabins. Both had sweatshirts tied around their waists.

"Are you ready for the campfire?" the taller girl asked.

"What campfire?" Alison blurted out, almost giving away the fact that the Magic Attic Club girls were strangers there.

The tall girl laughed. She had dark hair, freckles, and a wide grin. "How could you forget, Alison?" she said teasingly. "Once a week we get to cook dinner— it's the only time the food here actually tastes good!"

"Right," the other girl chimed in. She was petite, with short blond hair and green eyes. "Tonight we get to roast hot dogs and marshmallows and cook corn on the cob. Yum!" she added, rubbing her stomach playfully.

"Is that where you guys are headed?"Keisha asked. She noticed that the dark-haired girl's sweatshirt was embroidered with the name Rachel.

Rachel nodded. "First, Lindsay and I are going to the kitchen to get the hot dogs," she explained. "You're in the Evergreen cabin, right?"

"Yes," Rose answered hesitantly, hoping it was the right thing to say.

"It said on the job chart that the Evergreens are supposed to bring the marshmallows," Lindsay told them. "I think one of the cooks at the dining hall has them."

Rachel gave them a make-believe stern look. "You better not eat them all on the way, okay?"

"We'll see you in a few minutes," Lindsay called as she and Rachel left.

"Okay," Megan replied.

As soon as the two campers were out of sight, Heather turned to her friends. "A campfire," she said. "That sounds like fun, doesn't it?"

"I can't wait," Rose responded. "I love being outdoors in the woods, especially at night."

The Campfire

Megan patted Alison on the shoulder. "Are you still disappointed that we got here so late?" she asked.

"Not anymore," Alison replied. Now her blue eyes were filled with excitement. "I'm with Rose. I bet the campfire will be a blast!"

Heather was scanning the semicircle of cabins. "Can we find our cabin before we get the marshmallows at the dining hall? I want to see where we're going to sleep tonight." Then she noticed that the last cabin on the right was marked Evergreen.

Heather ran over and pushed open the door. Inside it was dark and cool. An unshaded lightbulb hung from the ceiling. When Heather flicked the switch, the girls saw a row of sturdy-looking cots with red sleeping bags unrolled on the mattresses. Lots of camping equipment was scattered around the bare floor: duffel bags, backpacks, rain gear, and several blue tennis rackets. Rose thought that the cabin smelled just like the woods, with the sweet scent of pine hanging in the air. Keisha laid the sleeping bag from the attic on one of the cots.

"Come on, you guys—we'd better get going, or we'll be late for dinner," Alison reminded them.

The girls quickly found the dining hall, picked up several plastic bags of marshmallows, and set out for the campfire pit.

By now darkness had fallen. Twice the girls headed in

the wrong direction, wound up on the deserted path to the lake, and had to turn back.

The second time it happened, Keisha was completely lost. "I have no idea where we are," she said, looking around in confusion.

"Me, either," Alison chimed in. "It's so dark out here."

Luckily, Rose had a better sense of direction. Within a few minutes, she'd found the right trail. "It's this way," she called, pointing to the right.

Relieved, Heather followed Rose. As she walked along, she heard a soft rustling in the bushes, as if an animal was exploring the trail, too.

"The woods are a little spooky at night, aren't they?" Heather remarked.

Alison and Megan both nodded, as if they'd been thinking the same thing.

"Oh, come on!" Rose laughed. "Once we get to know our way around better, the campgrounds won't be scary at all."

"I'm sure you're right," Heather murmured. "By tomorrow we'll be more familiar with the woods."

As they drew closer to the campfire, Keisha could

smell wood smoke and see the bright flames burning through the darkness.

"Hey! It's the marshmallow brigade!" Rachel called out as the five girls emerged from the woods.

Keisha grinned and held up the plastic bags. "I bet you're all happy to see us. We've got dessert!"

"We sure are glad you're here," one of the camp counselors said in a friendly voice. She was about twenty-five, blond, and dressed in olive-green shorts and a white sweatshirt. Her name tag read TINA. "Grab some sticks, girls, and make yourself some dinner."

About ten other girls were already seated on logs arranged in a circle around the campfire. Rose guessed that most of them were about her age. Many of the campers were cooking hot dogs, carefully holding their long sticks over the fire.

Rose and her friends found sticks and joined them. A tall, brown-haired counselor—Sharon, according to her name tag—was brushing ears of corn with butter, then wrapping them in aluminum foil for roasting on the fire. Rose couldn't wait to try the delicious-looking corn.

Before long the campers had stuffed themselves on all the food. Tina, the blond counselor, played a few songs on her guitar while the campers sang along. Then she laid down the instrument and announced that it was time for ghost stories.

"All right!" Alison cheered eagerly. "I know a really scary one!"

Megan had heard Alison's story about a ghostly hitchhiker before. As Alison began telling it, Megan leaned back and stared at the dark sky. It glittered with stars, and a nearly full moon hung above the tall pines that surrounded them. Perched in the branches of a distant tree, she thought she could make out the shadowy figure of a large owl.

This is fun, Megan thought contentedly. She had never gone camping before, and she was enjoying being outside in the cool night air and feeling the warm glow of the fire nearby.

After Alison finished telling her story, Rose told an eerie Native American tale that her father had told the winter before.

Next, Rachel raised her hand. "Can I tell one, too?" she asked the counselors.

"Sure, Rachel." Sharon grinned at her. "As long as you don't try to scare the new kids again this year with that one about the vampire!"

Everyone laughed. Megan wondered how long Rachel had been coming to Camp Whispering Pines—she certainly seemed to know everything about the place.

"I won't tell that one, Sharon," Rachel promised the dark haired counselor with a smile. "Actually—" her eyes briefly flicked across the fire, to where Megan was sitting with her friends—"I was thinking about telling the new campers about the ghost of Camp Whispering Pines."

"Oh, tell that one, Rachel," one of the girls pleaded. "It's so scary!"

"Okay," Rachel said, nodding. As she launched into the story, the five members of the Magic Attic Club leaned in closer to the fire to listen.

Chapter Four

THE GHOST OF CAMP WHISPERING PINES

A long time ago," Rachel began in a low voice, "a man named Ben Thorton built a cabin in these very woods."

"He was our camp director's great-grandfather, right?" a girl wearing a green T shirt interrupted her.

Rachel nodded. The flames from the fire sent eerie shadows flickering across her cheeks.

"Ben Thorton loved to hunt in the woods and fish in the lake. Sometimes when he came to the woods he brought along his grandson, Jacob, who was only five

35

years old.

"Then one day tragedy struck. There was a terrible train wreck out west. Jacob's parents were on board the train, and they were instantly killed."

"That's so sad," Megan whispered. A couple of others murmured their agreement.

"Little Jacob came to live with his grandfather, who loved him very much. But for months, poor Jacob was in shock. He was so grief-stricken over the loss of his parents, he wouldn't talk. He never said a word—except to Ben's hunting dog, an old hound named Blue.

"When summer came, Ben decided to bring Jacob to the woods. He thought the fresh air would help the boy forget about his grief, even for just a little while."

Just then Sharon leaned forward and poked the fire with a long stick. The embers scattered into the dark sky and extinguished themselves.

"After just a day or two in the woods," Rachel went on, "Jacob was like a brand-new person. He still wasn't talking, but one day Ben actually heard him laugh while he was playing with Blue. Every day he and Blue had a great time romping in the woods and playing in the cave at the foot of Boulder Hill."

Rachel drew in her breath. "Then tragedy struck again. One night there was a violent thunderstorm. Blue had always hated thunder."

"My dog hates it, too!" one of the younger campers interrupted.

"Sssssh," Lindsay said, motioning for the girl to be quiet.

"That night Blue seemed especially nervous," Rachel continued. "It was as if he knew that something terrible was going to happen. All night long, he paced up and down, up and down, in the tiny cabin. And then it began to rain—and rain hard.

"When Ben opened the door to look outside, the dog darted out into the darkness. "Blue!" Jacob yelled after him, then, before Ben could stop him, he took off after the dog. Ben ran after them, but the boy and the dog were gone. It was as if the dark, stormy night had just swallowed them up."

Megan felt Alison tightly grip her arm. "Did Ben ever find them?" Alison asked.

"Well," Rachel went on. "Ben searched the woods that night. He checked the cave where Blue and Jacob liked to play, and he went all around the lake looking for them. But there was no trace of either of them. Until one night"—Rachel lowered her voice to a whisper—"Ben heard a sound outside his cabin. At first he thought it was the wind rustling the pine trees. But then he realized that someone was crying—a little boy was moaning in pain.

"Ben rushed outside, desperately hoping to find his grandson. But as he drew closer..." Rachel let her voice trail off for a second, and Heather felt her body tense. "Ben realized it wasn't Jacob, after all. It was—"

"Who was it?" Heather burst out.

"His ghost!"

Someone gasped. "His ghost?"

"Yes. It was his ghost," Rachel said solemnly. Her brown eyes looked huge in the firelight as she stared at Heather and her friends. "And to this day, whenever there's a thunderstorm, Jacob's ghost still haunts the woods, looking for his lost dog."

It was late when the counselors announced it was time to put out the fire and head back to the cabins. The Magic Attic girls stayed behind to help Sharon and Tina pack up the leftover food and supplies. Then, after saying goodnight to the two counselors, the five made their way through the dark woods.

Heather was glad she was wearing a sweater. The wind had picked up, and the air felt chilly.

"Rachel's story was pretty creepy, wasn't it?" Megan said.

"It was sad, too," Heather remarked. Even though she was still wearing her warm red sweater, she felt a shiver ripple through her. "Do you think it's true?"

No one answered her for a moment.

Alison glanced nervously at the high branches looming over them as the trees swayed in the breeze. "I think it *is* true," she said softly.

"I don't," Rose chimed in. "I think Rachel just enjoys scaring people."

"I agree," Keisha added. "Didn't you hear Sharon warn her not to spook the new campers?"

"Yes, but the way Rachel told the story, it sounded so real," Alison insisted. "She even said that Ben Thorton was the camp director's great-grandfather."

"So?" Keisha still wasn't convinced. "She could have just made up that part, Ali. Mr. Thorton wasn't at the campfire, so he couldn't deny it."

"I guess," Megan replied. "But—"

Wooooooooo. Just then a soft moan filled the night air.

Megan froze in her tracks. "What was that?" she whispered.

"It's the ghost!" Alison whispered back.

"No way," Keisha said. "We're in the wilderness, remember? It's probably an animal or something."

"Moaning like that?" Heather replied. "I don't think so."

"I think I saw an owl when we were at the campfire,"

Megan said uneasily. "Maybe it's him."

Woooooooooooo.

The sound came again, and Alison listened more carefully. "You really don't think it's the ghost, do you, Keisha?" she asked.

"Absolutely not," Keisha answered.

"It's probably an owl, like Megan said, " Rose piped up. "Besides, it's a beautiful, clear night. Didn't Rachel say that the ghost only shows up when it rains?"

Megan nodded, suddenly feeling foolish for thinking that the woods might be haunted. "I guess we got a little carried away by Rachel's story," she said.

Keisha nodded. "Trust me—there's no ghost around here."

The girls dropped the subject as they continued toward their cabin. When they arrived, they changed into their camp nightshirts and slipped into their sleeping bags. Rose and Keisha quickly fell sound asleep. But for a long time, Megan, Alison, and Heather lay awake in the darkness, still thinking about ghosts and wondering if a little boy had truly disappeared in the woods one night.

Outside their cabin, the chilly breeze made the trees rustle and moan.

Chapter
Five

A BUSY DAY

y seven forty-five the next morning, the girls were in the dining hall eating breakfast with the other campers.

"Rachel was right." Keisha made a face as she looked up from the stack of pancakes on her plate. "The food here is awful."

"My pancakes taste like rubber," Rose agreed.

Megan raised her eyebrows. "Yours are that good?" she joked. "I poured maple syrup all over mine, and I still can't eat them."

Just then Heather noticed a tall man dressed in khaki shorts and a white T shirt standing in the center of the room. He was waving to get everyone's attention.

"Hey, Mr. Thorton," a camper yelled. "Where were you last night? We were telling ghost stories around the fire."

"Sorry I missed it," the gray-haired man said. He wore a baseball cap printed with the camp's logo. "My daughter and her family arrived last night from out of town. They're going to be spending a few days with us."

"Do they have to eat at the dining hall, too?" Rachel joked. "Or are you going to take them *out* for dinner?"

Megan wondered if the camp director would be annoyed by Rachel's crack. But instead he just laughed, as if he were used to jokes. Then he motioned again for all the campers to be quiet.

When the room was finally silent, Mr. Thorton began going over the schedule for the day. "This morning we're going to split up for activities," he explained. "Then this afternoon at two, we'll meet outside the rec hall for a scavenger hunt."

"All right!" Keisha flashed a thumbs-up at her friends. "That sounds like fun."

Sharon had joined Mr. Thorton in the center of the room.

A Busy Day

"We'll tell you a little more about the hunt this afternoon," she said. "Right now I want you to finish your breakfast, and then head over to the chart—she pointed to a bulletin board posted on the wall—to sign up for two activities. You can play tennis, do crafts, go boating, play volleyball, get in some more archery practice. Or you can sign up for cleanup duty if you'd rather," she added with a grin.

When she and Mr. Thorton had finished speaking, the Magic Attic girls dumped the remains of their breakfast in the trash, then examined the chart more closely. Keisha, Alison, and Rose decided to head to the archery course, then go canoeing on the lake. Megan and Heather signed up for tennis, followed by a session at the crafts hut; they were both looking forward to making friendship bracelets and dreamcatchers.

After their busy morning and a lunch of soup and cold grilled-cheese sandwiches, the five friends met outside the rec hall. It was a little before two o'clock, and all of the campers were beginning to assemble for the scavenger hunt. Alison had never been on one before. "How does it work, anyway?" she asked.

Megan explained. "First, the counselors will divide us

into teams. Each team gets a list of things they have to find. The winners are the first team that makes it back to camp with everything on the list."

"I hope my team wins!" Alison declared.

Her friends laughed. They all knew how much Alison loved sports and games, and how much she loved to win.

"Okay, campers," Sharon called out when she and Mr. Thorton arrived at the rec hall. "Who's ready to go?"

"We are!" everyone seemed to shout at once.

Keisha grinned at the girls' enthusiasm. Then she crossed her fingers for luck as Sharon began forming teams. I hope I'm with my friends, she thought.

"Team number one," the counselor called, "the Evergreens. Team number two…"

"Yes!" Alison whispered. "We're on the same team!"

The five girls smiled as they slapped high fives, glad to be together for the hunt.

When Sharon finished announcing the teams, Tina and Mr. Thorton handed each group a sketched map of the campgrounds, a list of objects they were supposed to find, and a jar with holes poked in the lid.

"What's this for?" Rachel asked.

Mr. Thorton smiled. "Check your list," he said.

Rose quickly scanned the sheet of paper while her friends read it over her shoulder:

1) a wildflower

2) moss growing on a rock near Thorton's Creek

3) a feather

4) a leaf from a deciduous tree

5) 4 pinecones

6) bark from the birch tree near the elbow in the creek

7) an insect (you can place it in the jar and we'll free it after the hunt)

9) a vine (make sure it's not poison ivy!)

10) a surprise

"So that's what the jar's for," Megan said, making a

face. "We have to bring back a bug."

Alison grimaced, too. "Maybe we'll get lucky and find a ladybug or something."

Megan nodded. "I don't mind touching *them*," she said.

"What's a deciduous tree?" Keisha asked, looking at the list again.

"It's a tree that loses its leaves in the fall," Rose explained. "Some of these things might be hard to find, but I've seen plenty of oak and maple trees around."

"I wonder what they mean by 'a surprise,'" Heather commented.

Sharon overheard her. "We want you to bring back something from the woods that you didn't expect to find."

Rachel nodded. "That was on the list last year, too. Our cabin found part of a cardinal's egg," she added. "It was really neat."

Once each team had a list and a map, Sharon explained a few more rules. "Work together, and use your maps," she said. "And I want everyone to be back at camp no later than four-thirty." Her expression looked serious.

"Did everyone remember to put rain gear in their backpacks?" Mr. Thorton asked suddenly.

The Magic Attic girls shook their heads. So did most of the other campers.

"Why do we need our ponchos, Mr. Thorton?" Megan asked.

"It's not unusual to have a sudden thunderstorm

around here at this time of year," the camp director replied. Then he smiled. "And I like my campers to be prepared for any crisis," he added.

The campers who didn't have their rain gear rushed back to their cabins to get it, then quickly returned to the rec hall. Rose was stuffing her yellow poncho into her backpack when Sharon picked up the whistle she wore around her neck.

"Ready, campers?" Sharon yelled.

"Yes!" everyone shouted at once. The Magic Attic girls shouted loudest of all. Then Sharon blew her whistle— and the scavenger hunt began!

C h a p t e r

Six

THE SCAVENGER HUNT

The teams rushed away from the rec hall and into the woods, where everyone quickly scattered. Heather stopped to look at the map.

"Where should we go first, Heather?" Megan asked.

"Why don't we try to locate the creek?" Rose suggested. "We're supposed to find a rock with moss growing on it there, plus get some bark from a birch tree."

"That's a good idea, Rose," Keisha agreed. "On our way, we can look for the rest of the stuff on the list."

Before long Megan spotted something nestled in a bed of pine needles. "Cross out number five," she called gleefully to Alison, who was holding the list. "I just found some pinecones!"

Twenty minutes later Keisha found wildflowers with yellow and orange blossoms sprouting from the ground near an old tree stump.

"I think these are what Aunt Frances calls butter-and-eggs," Heather said as she and Megan bent down to pick a few sprigs. "She showed me some on a trip we took once." They handed them to Rose, who tucked them safely into her backpack.

The girls were still searching for the creek when Alison noticed a tall tree with a thick grayish trunk and lots of broad green leaves clinging to its branches. She glanced at Rose. "That's an oak, right?"

"Right. And it's deciduous," Rose replied.

"Good. I'll get a leaf," Alison said, hurrying over to the tree.

As she reached up to pluck one from a low-growing branch, she spotted a field in the distance. It was very overgrown with grass and weeds, as if no one had been there for a long time. Then something else caught her eye. Poking up from the ground were five or six large stones.

They're tombstones! Alison realized. A shiver crept up

her spine.

"Hey, you guys," she called, frantically waving her friends over to her. "You've got to see this!"

Megan gasped when she saw the stones. "I didn't notice a cemetery on the map."

"There isn't one," Heather said, checking the paper quickly.

Keisha was intrigued. "That looks pretty interesting," she said. "Do you think we have time to take a look at it?"

"I think so," Rose replied, looking at her watch. "It's only a little after three o'clock, and we've already found three things on our list. We don't have to be back for another hour and a half."

As the girls approached the cemetery, Megan could see that the stones marking the graves were old and crumbling. They had obviously been there for a long time.

Heather stood in front of one of the stones. She was startled when she read the inscription:

BENJAMIN RAYMOND THORTON
1831 - 1901

"Whoa." Heather sounded hoarse. "I bet this is the Ben Thorton from Rachel's story!"

Megan nodded as she came over to see for herself. "There really was someone named Ben Thorton."

Alison glanced around at the other tombstones. All of the people buried in this small cemetery had the last name Thorton; that meant they were all related to Mr. Thorton, the camp director.

One small gray stone stood apart from the rest, with tall weeds covering its inscription. Megan bent down to push away the overgrowth. When she read the name chiseled into the stone, she felt her heart skip a beat.

JACOB THORTON
1881 - 1887

"Look!" Megan called to her friends. "There was a Jacob Thorton, too! And he was only six years old when he died."

"Didn't Rachel say that Jacob was five when he disappeared?" Keisha asked.

"I'm pretty sure she did," Rose said. She knew that Alison, Megan, and Heather believed Rachel's story, but she was very skeptical. "These tombstones don't necessarily mean that Rachel was telling the truth about a ghost," she said to her friends. "For all we know,

Rachel's seen the cemetery, too, and she used the names on these stones to make up her ghost story."

"Rose is right," Keisha added. "Finding this cemetery doesn't prove anything."

Megan didn't want to argue with her friends, so she didn't say anything more. But inside her stomach felt hollow. Had young Jacob Thorton really disappeared in the woods like that? She wished she knew the answer.

Heather looked pale and worried. "Let's get out of here," she said suddenly. She stepped away from the graves, and the others followed. "Let's go finish the scavenger hunt."

By the time they reached the creek, the girls had found a bright blue feather, a small, dark beetle, and an ivylike vine that had been tightly wound around the branches of tall bush.

"We still need the mossy rock and the bark from the birch tree," Rose said.

"And number ten—the surprise," Keisha reminded her.

"Oh, right," Rose mumbled. "I forgot about that for a minute."

"Doesn't a graveyard count as a surprise?" Alison blurted out.

"We can't exactly take that back to camp," Rose replied, smiling.

Alison shrugged. Rose seemed able to shake off their discovery, but it was all that Alison could think about. What had happened to little Jacob Thorton?

Tall trees lined the banks of the creek. The girls stood near the edge and looked closely at the rocks.

"There's a stone with some moss on it," Heather said, pointing to one covered with some green, fuzzy-looking growth. As she knelt to pick it up, she decided to test the temperature of the clear water.

"Yikes!" she cried, pulling back her hand. "It's freezing!"

Heather was so startled by the cold that she didn't notice when the map fell out of her pocket.

"The map, Heather!" Keisha yelled. "Grab the map! It's in the creek!"

"Oh, no!" Frantically, Heather tried to scoop up the piece of paper, but it had already drifted out of her reach. Not far ahead the water widened to about ten or eleven feet. "I can't reach it without going in," Heather called out helplessly.

"I'll get it," Rose said. She snapped a long branch off a nearby tree. Quickly, she leaned over and fished out the map.

Rose shook out the folded sheet of paper. But to her dismay it had ripped in two places. And the water had blurred the ink so much it was unreadable.

"Uh-oh," Megan murmured. "Do you think we can find our way back to camp on our own?"

"Sure," Alison said, trying to sound more confident than she felt. "Why don't we follow the creek and see if we can find the 'elbow' near the birch tree. Then we can figure out how to get back."

Her friends agreed. No one knew what else to do, so

they began following her

Rose giggled as she suddenly thought of something. "What a weird word to use—an *elbow* in the creek."

"I know," Alison agreed, laughing as she turned around to look at Rose. "I wonder if the creek has a hip!"

"What about a shoulder?" Keisha joined in.

Heather shook her head and smiled. "You guys are acting pretty goofy."

Rose laughed again. "It's a survival technique for campers who are lost in the woods."

Megan figured they'd been walking for about thirty minutes when she glanced at her watch. It was already four-fifteen.

We've been following the creek through the woods for a long time now, she thought, worried. We're never going to make it back to camp by four-thirty.

As they headed deeper into the forest, the air felt damp and chilly. Glancing up at the sky, Megan saw no trace of the sun. She felt her pulse quicken. She turned around to face her friends. "Is it me," she asked, "or is it suddenly getting a lot darker?"

"Relax, Megan," Keisha replied." It just seems darker here because the woods are so dense."

Megan nodded, but she was still worried. She had the terrible feeling that they were headed in the wrong direction. She didn't want to think about how far they'd wandered from camp.

Rose felt uneasy, too. "This can't be right," she said, suddenly stopping. "I haven't seen any birch trees or any bends in the creek."

Alison nodded. "I think we're lost," she said, echoing Megan's thoughts.

"What are we going to do?" Heather asked with a sigh.

Up ahead Megan spotted a rocky hill. She thought she remembered hearing something about it. Was it on the map? She tried to remember, but she couldn't.

As the girls nervously looked around, thunder rumbled through the woods.

The sound startled Alison. "I think it's going to rain," she said as a jagged bolt of lightning split the sky. Suddenly she was filled with a sense of foreboding.

"Oh, no," Heather said. Things were going from bad to worse.

"We'd better put on our ponchos," Rose said, trying to stay calm. As she pulled her rain gear out of her backpack, she was glad that Mr. Thorton had reminded them to bring it. It looked like they were going to need it.

Just then thunder boomed again, this time making Keisha and Megan jump. The five girls looked at one another, their eyes wide.

Heather glanced upward. High above them, dark, threatening clouds scudded across the sky. As the storm drew closer all she could think about was Jacob Thorton. The little boy had disappeared in the woods during a summer thunderstorm just like this one.

What are we going to do? Heather wondered. She felt the knot in her stomach tighten.

Chapter

Seven

INSIDE THE CAVE

ightning ripped through the
sky again.

Rose nervously eyed the storm
clouds hovering over them. "We'd
better find a safer place than right
here," she said to her friends. "It's
very dangerous to stand under
the trees when there's lightning
like this."

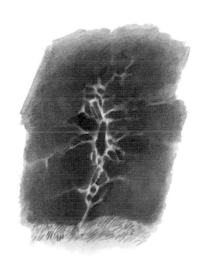

Megan's gaze flicked again to the rocky hill ahead, and something clicked inside her brain: Rachel had mentioned a cave at the foot of a rocky hill in her ghost story! That must be the one she'd been talking about.

Just then rain began to pour from the sky. The wind picked up quickly, swirling the leaves that lay scattered on the ground.

"Come on, you guys!" Megan had to shout to be heard over the sound of the rain and another clap of thunder. "I think I know where we can find shelter!" With that, she raced toward the hill, and her friends followed.

Sure enough, when they reached the foot of the slope, Megan spotted a wide gap in the rocks.

"It's a cave!" Rose called out. "Wow, Megan. How did you know this was here?"

"Rachel's story," Megan said. "At least *part* of it was true. She said that this was where Jacob and Blue liked to play together."

The girls ducked into the cave and shook off their dripping ponchos.

"Yuck!" Rose exclaimed. "My shoes are soaked."

The cave was so dark that Alison couldn't tell how big it was. She blinked, trying to get her eyes used to the darkness. She was glad to be out of the rain, but it was a little creepy in the cave. It smelled moldy, and the floor was slick with moisture.

Heather gazed around with wide eyes. "Don't bats live in caves?" she asked, not sure she wanted to hear the answer.

Keisha nodded. "Sometimes," she admitted. "But they're nocturnal. Maybe they're all still asleep."

The girls took a few steps, then stopped. Ahead, the cave narrowed and split off into two small tunnels. They decided to stay where they were, close to the opening, and sat down on the damp floor. From somewhere ahead, they heard a sound they couldn't identify.

"I'm starved," Heather said, trying to distract herself from her spooky thoughts.

Everyone laughed, glad to have something else to think about.

"So am I," Alison chimed in. "I didn't eat my pancakes at breakfast, and that alphabet soup we had for lunch was even worse."

"Is that what it was?" Keisha joked. "I thought it was dishwater!"

Rose reached into her backpack and pulled out her flashlight. "I know I have some snacks in here," she said, shining the light into the bag.

"I have a few granola bars in mine," Megan said.

"And I have peanuts," Keisha chimed in.

"I don't have any food" Alison said as she peered into her backpack. "But I have this…" She grinned as she held up a small compass.

"That's great, Ali," Keisha said, relieved. "Now once the rain stops, we can find our way back to camp."

The girls split the snacks into five servings. It was very quiet as everyone munched away.

"Mmmm," Alison said, biting into a raspberry granola bar. "I—"An odd sound rang out from the depths of the cave, and she froze, listening carefully.

It's just water or something, she told herself. But a moment later, the sound came again, and this time she knew it wasn't water.

Megan's eyes were wide with panic. "Someone's crying!" she whispered.

"It's the ghost!" Heather gasped.

Stay calm, Rose told herself. But as she got to her feet, she could feel her heart thumping inside her chest. She scanned the cave with her flashlight and took a few steps deeper into the darkness. Then she shone the light straight ahead, where the cave narrowed into the two wormlike tunnels. Both were so narrow, Rose knew she couldn't walk through; she'd have to crawl.

The sobbing sound echoed once more. And this time it was closer, Rose realized. Her chest felt tight, and she could hardly catch her breath. Her friends stood behind her as Rose shined her light into the tunnel on the left. She couldn't see anything but empty darkness. When she shifted the beam to the other tunnel, she gasped. Huddled inside the narrow passageway was a small, dark figure. Its eyes glowed like tiny balls of light.

Heather let out a frightened, choked sound, and Megan gasped. Rose felt her own hands tremble. The light shook as she kept it trained straight ahead.

Finally Rose took a shaky breath and forced herself to really look at the figure in the tunnel. It looked like a little boy dressed in jeans and a dark T shirt. Tears were streaming down his cheeks, and his eyes looked terrified.

Then a hoarse voice came from the tunnel, echoing softly through the cave and jolting Rose like an electrical shock;

"My name is Jacob. And I can't find my dog or my grandfather."

Chapter
Eight

MORE
MYSTERIES

lison stared at the little boy. She felt her legs
wobble as if they were made out of jelly.

"It's the ghost!" Megan shouted. "Let's go!"

The five girls whirled around and raced out of the cave
and into the rain. They ran until they reached a clearing a
short distance away.

Rose was so shaken, she could hardly speak. "I can't
believe it," she whispered. "I can't believe there's really a
ghost in there!"

The rain was still coming down hard.

"Come on," Megan urged her friends. "Let's get back to camp."

"We can't," Alison replied in a small voice.

They all looked at her. "Why not, Ali?" Heather asked.

"I left my backpack inside the cave. The compass is in it."

"Oh no," Megan murmured. Now they'd have to figure out how to get back on their own. She tried to think clearly for a minute. "We started out heading north," she said. "Then I think we turned—"

Keisha interrupted her. "I'm going back in there," she announced.

"You can't!" Heather exclaimed. "It's not safe!"

"You saw the ghost, too, Keisha," Alison chimed in.

But all Keisha could think about was how little the figure had looked. Somehow, it had reminded her of her sister, Ashley. What if Ashley were alone, lost in the woods somewhere?

"I'm not sure if that was really a ghost," she told her friends. "But it looked so—I don't know—scared. I can't just leave without knowing."

"But, Keisha," Rose replied. "We don't know *what* that was. What if—"

Before Rose could finish, Keisha turned around and ran back into the cave.

"We can't let her go in there alone!" Alison cried.

Without stopping to think, the four girls took off after their friend.

"Keisha!" Megan shouted.

Rose still held her flashlight. She shone it ahead of them. "Keisha?" she called out.

There was no reply from their friend. But just then Rose heard another familiar voice.

"Anybody in here?"

Hopeful, she turned around. Sure enough, Mr. Thorton appeared behind her. Sharon was standing beside him.

"We're here!" Rose called back.

Sharon sighed. "I'm so glad we found you girls!"

Relief flooded over Megan. "We're so glad you found us, too!" she said, hurrying over to Mr. Thorton and the counselor. "Our map got ruined, and then it started to rain. We were pretty scared."

"Good thing you found the cave," Mr. Thorton said.

"Yes, but. . . We also found the ghost!" Heather blurted out.

"What?" Mr. Thorton's eyes grew wide with surprise. "What are you talking about?"

"Jacob," Heather murmured. "He's in the cave. Keisha went after him," she added, wondering if anything she was saying made any sense.

But to her surprise, Mr. Thorton's expression had

turned from confusion to relief.

"What?" he cried. "Jacob's here, too? You found my grandson?"

"Your grandson?" Rose echoed. "But Jacob's not your grandson," she began. "He's—"

"Hey!" Keisha cried, stepping out of the darkness. Rose couldn't believe her eyes: Keisha was holding the little boy's hand.

"Grandpa!" the boy shouted.

Megan watched in amazement as the child ran to Mr. Thorton and hugged him hard.

"You gave us such a scare, Jake," Mr. Thorton murmured, holding the boy tightly. "Your mom and dad are going to be very happy to see you. They waited back at camp in case you showed up there."

Jacob was crying. "I lost Buddy, Grandpa," he sobbed. "Remember when he chased a chipmunk and ran away in the woods? I ran after him, but I couldn't find him."

"Guess what, Jake?" Mr. Thorton said softly. "Buddy's back at camp. He found his way back there all on his own."

"He did!" Jacob's expression turned to delight.

Rose looked helplessly at Sharon. "What's going on?" she asked.

"I'm so confused," Alison put in.

"Jacob is Mr. Thorton's grandson," Sharon explained. "He's visiting for a few days, and this afternoon he got lost in the woods, too. He and Mr. Thorton were taking a walk when Jake took off after Buddy."

"You mean, Jacob's not a ghost?" Alison said in disbelief.

"A ghost?" Sharon echoed. "What in the world made you girls think...?" Then a light of recognition sparked in her eyes. Her loud laughter rang through the cave. "Oh, no. You believed that crazy story of Rachel's, didn't you?"

Megan nodded sheepishly.

Heather was still confused. "But how did Rachel know about Jacob Thorton?" she asked Sharon.

"I don't think she knows about this Jacob," Sharon explained, motioning to Mr. Thorton's grandson. "His last name is O'Neill, anyway. But Rachel's been coming to the camp for years," she went on with a shrug. "She's probably seen Jacob Thorton's tombstone in the cemetery and decided to use his name in her ghost story." Sharon shook her head. "Rachel does this every year. Every summer she manages to scare some new campers half to death."

"I feel so stupid," Alison groaned.

Megan had another question for Sharon. "But last night, I did hear someone moaning in the woods," she said. "Who was making that sound, if it wasn't a ghost?"

Sharon smiled again. "It's the wind," she explained. "Sometimes on breezy nights, it sounds like a human cry."

"So, that's why the camp is called Whispering Pines, isn't it?" Megan asked.

"Exactly," Sharon told her.

When they arrived back at camp, Sharon and Mr. Thorton took Jacob to see his worried parents. The girls headed for their cabin, soaking wet and exhausted.

"I feel so stupid for thinking Jacob was a ghost," Heather said. "But I'm really glad he's safe."

Rose agreed. "His parents are going to be thrilled to see him."

"I just thought of something," Alison said with a grin. "We're probably the only ones on the scavenger hunt who found a missing person in the woods!"

"You're right, Ali," Rose agreed, starting up the steps in front of their cabin. "We never did find number six on our list, the birch bark, but we did find number ten—a surprise."

Just then Rachel darted out of her cabin next door.

"Are you okay?" she called. "We were all so worried about you when you disappeared like that."

Megan was definitely not glad to see Rachel. "Thanks a lot, Rachel," she said sarcastically. She was about to tell her off for making up that story, but Alison cut her off.

"That was a pretty good ghost story you told us, Rachel," Alison said, laughing. "When we were lost in the woods, we actually thought we saw the ghost."

"You scared us half to death!" Heather put in.

"I did?" Rachel grinned, but a moment later her expression turned apologetic. "Sorry about that. I was just fooling around."

"Well, you fooled us," Rose remarked. "I can't believe that even I thought we'd bumped into the ghost of Whispering Pines!"

As everyone laughed, Megan felt her anger melt away. Rachel had scared them, but she'd also made the scavenger hunt more exciting. Believing in ghost stories was silly, but in a way it was fun, too.

"The cook saved you guys some food, if you're hungry," Rachel said.

"We're starving," Rose said warily. "But what was for dinner?"

"Texas tamales," Rachel said, screwing up her face. "They were awful!" With a big grin, she waved good-bye and continued on her way to the rec hall, where some of the campers were playing board games.

The girls went into their cabin. "You know what?" Megan said. "I think I'm ready to go home."

"Me, too," Rose chimed in. "I think my mom is making chicken salad for dinner. I'd much rather eat that."

More Mysteries

Heather, Keisha, and Alison were ready to return home, too. As they stood in front of the mirror, Heather whispered, "Good-bye, Camp Whispering Pines."

A moment later, they were back in Ellie's attic.

"How's your book, Ellie?" Keisha called as the girls trooped back onto the porch and sat down.

"Oh, it's wonderful," Ellie said enthusiastically. "I'm almost finished with it. And how was your adventure, girls?" she asked, setting aside the book.

"We had so much fun, Ellie!" Heather said enthusiastically. "We played tennis and made friendship bracelets, and—"

"We went boating and hiking," Rose chimed in.

"And some of us thought we met a ghost," Alison added. Together she and her friends told Ellie about the "ghost" of Jacob Thorton.

Ellie chuckled. "Sometimes it's fun to believe in spooky things," she said, patting the book beside her. "That's why I'm enjoying this mystery so much. It's suspenseful, and even scary in a few spots."

Megan nodded. After being silly enough to believe in the ghost of Camp Whispering Pines, she knew exactly what Ellie meant. Being scared *had* been fun—at least for a little while.

Heather laughed. "Well, we don't believe in ghosts

anymore, Ellie," she remarked. "Now that all the excitement is over, we'll all go back to being bored stiff."

"I'm not so sure about that." There was a bright gleam in Ellie's blue eyes. "I want to show you all something," she said, reaching inside her book and pulling out the pink sheet of paper she'd been using for a bookmark. "I spotted this at the library yesterday, and thought it might be something that you'd enjoy."

"What is it?" Alison asked curiously.

Ellie handed over the slip.

Keisha read it aloud: "Calling All Kids! Are you a fan of mysteries and spooky ghost stories? Do you enjoy thrills and chills? Join the library's new summer book club. We'll read and talk about lots of great mysteries for the rest of the summer."

"That sounds great," Megan said eagerly.

"If you want to sign up, you'd better do it fast," Ellie said. "I think the deadline is today."

Megan glanced at her watch. It was four-fifteen. If they hurried, they could make it to the library in the nick of time.

"Come on," Keisha said, rushing for the door.

"See you soon, Ellie!" Rose called.

"'Bye!" Heather and Alison

said at the same time.

"Thank you, Ellie," Megan said softly as she followed her friends out the door.

"You're welcome, Megan," Ellie said. She smiled as she turned back to her book.

In front of Ellie's house, Megan hopped on her bike and began pedaling toward the library behind her friends. It was still boiling hot, but Megan barely noticed. All she could think about was signing up for the new mystery book club.

If you enjoyed this book, be sure to look for these other Magic Attic Club adventures!

The Group Adventures:
The Secret of the Attic
Trapped Beyond the Magic Attic

Alison

Alison Goes for the Gold
Alison on the Trail
Alison Saves the Wedding
Alison Walks the Wire
Alison of Arabia

Heather

Heather at the Barre
Heather, Belle of the Ball
Heather Takes the Reins
Viva Heather!
Heather Goes to Hollywood

Fun, Friends, Imagination & Adventure

Keisha

Three Cheers for Keisha
Keisha the Fairy Snow Queen
Keisha Leads the Way
Keisha to the Rescue
Keisha's Maze Mystery

Megan

Princess Megan
Cowgirl Megan
Downhill Megan
Megan's Masquerade
Megan's Balancing Act

Rose

Rose's Magic Touch
Rose Faces the Music
Cheyenne Rose